ISBN 978-0-9681025-8-9

PRINTED IN CANADA

I BOX
Publishing

PROLOGUE

HM.
-WELL, IT'S BEEN A **LONG TIME**, AFTER ALL.
-I THINK I MIGHT HAVE BEEN HIDING.
-THEN I SLEPT FOR A WHILE...
IT'S ALL A BIT FOGGY NOW.
-NOBODY **FOLLOWED** YOU, DID THEY?
I DON'T THINK SO.
IT FILLS ME WITH REGRET TO REPORT THAT **LOW TIMES** HAVE FALLEN UPON THE **QUEEN OF THE GALAXY**.
GOSH.
-THAT'S VERY SAD.
I AGREE.
HOLD ON!
-I'LL BE STRAIGHT BACK!
?
...
I BROUGHT SMOOTHIES!
OOOH.
HOW THOUGHTFUL!
BLUP BLUP!
IF YOU **BLOW**, YOU CAN MAKE BUBBLES.
LOW TIMES UNDER A HEDGE AREN'T SO BAD WHEN YOU CAN SHARE SMOOTHIES.

CHAPTER ONE

"THE HEDGE WITCH"

EEEW!
YOU EAT BUGS?
YES.
THEY ARE CRUNCHY AND BITTER.
--FOOD FOR THE SOUL!
-I HAVE A TORMENTED SOUL, YOU SEE.
THAT'S AWFUL!
IT IS MY LOT IN LIFE.
BUT I ENDURE.
BUT THE QUEEN OF THE GALAXY SHOULDN'T BE LIVING UNDER A HEDGE AT ALL.
YOU'D THINK THAT, WOULDN'T YOU?
-BUT I GREW COMPLACENT, AND THEN.., BETRAYAL!
-NOW SELF-SERVING MAD MEN RUN AMOK IN THE HALLS OF POWER!
IT IS ALL VERY DIRE.
THEY WOULD CUT OFF MY HEAD IF THEY EVER FOUND ME!
-YOU MUSTN'T TELL ANYBODY I AM HERE!
OOOOH.
REALLY..?
WHAT IS IT?
I THINK I MIGHT HAVE DONE SOMETHING TERRIBLE.
WHAT? ALREADY?
HOW IS THAT EVEN POSSIBLE?
DAD SAYS I HAVE A KNACK FOR IT.
-THAT'S WHY HE SENT ME TO STAY HERE WITH MY AUNT AND UNCLE.
-TO "SEE WHO'D BE LAUGHING THEN".
OH MY.

I'M SORRY!
YOU TOLD THE KITCHEN STAFF ABOUT ME..?!
I'M DOOMED!
WHEN THE COOK MADE SMOOTHIES FOR US, HE ASKED WHO I WAS SHARING THEM WITH.
BAH! KITCHEN STAFF!
-THEY CHATTER
THEY TELL EVERYBODY!
KITCHENS ARE A SECURITY NIGHTMARE!
-YOU CAN CONTROL EVERY OTHER PART OF A PALACE, BUT PEOPLE STILL NEED FOOD.
RRR!
THIS IS WHY I EAT BUGS!
-SO IT'S REALLY BAD THEN?
IT'S WORSE THAN BAD!
I'LL BE DISCOVERED!
-MY ENEMIES WILL FINALLY HAVE ME VAPORIZED!!
OOOOOOH!
I'M SORRY!
CAN I HELP MAKE IT BETTER?
PROBABLY NOT.
MY ENEMIES ARE RUTHLESS!
OH, WOE.
-AS IF LIVING UNDER A HEDGE WASN'T BAD ENOUGH!
ASHEEEELLE!
DINNER TIME!
YIKES!
BAH!
IT'S THAT ACCURSED COOK!
-NOW THE ARMY WILL BE AFTER ME!

COMING!
"AN ARMY MARCHES ON IT'S STOMACH" IT'S STOMACH!
-COOKS CONTROL THE EMPIRE! IT'S A CONSPIRACY OF CHEFS!
WELL, YOU CAN'T STAY HERE IN THE GARDEN NOW THAT THEY KNOW.
-I'LL HAVE TO HIDE YOU SOMEPLACE ELSE.
WHERE?
UM... MAYBE IN MY CLOSET WHILE EVERY-BODY IS HAVING DINNER.
THEN AT NIGHT, YOU CAN TAKE ONE OF THE SHIPS AND FLY AWAY.
HM... THAT'S ACTUALLY NOT A BAD PLAN.
-I ALWAYS SAID YOU'D BE A BRIGHT GIRL.
I'M COMING OUT.
OKAY. -LET'S GO.
ARE YOU CERTAIN YOU'RE THE QUEEN OF THE GALAXY?
YES!! WHY DOES EVERYBODY KEEP ASKING ME THAT?

UGH!
-AND JUST LOOK AT THIS HORRID, DISGUSTING LITTLE BODY!
YOU DON'T LOOK THAT BAD.
STOP TRYING TO CONSOLE ME!
-MY BRAIN HAS BEEN TRANSPLANTED INTO SOME KIND OF WEIRD SPACE-ELF!
IT'S A DISASTER!
-HOLD ON.
YOU MEAN THAT'S NOT YOUR REAL BODY..?
-IS THAT EVEN POSSIBLE?
SURE, WHY NOT?
-WHEN YOU'RE QUEEN OF THE GALAXY, ALL MANNER OF SECRET TECHNOLOGIES ARE AT YOUR DISPOSAL.
GOSH!
BUT WHY DID YOU DECIDE TO BE A SPACE-ELF?
HOW SHOULD I KNOW?
-HECK, I'VE BEEN LIVING UNDER A HEDGE EATING BUGS!
WELL, I GUESS AT LEAST THIS WAY NOBODY WILL RECOGNIZE YOU.
MAYBE THAT'S WHY I PICKED A SPACE-ELF
-TO FOIL MY ENEMIES.
SCRITCH
HMM...

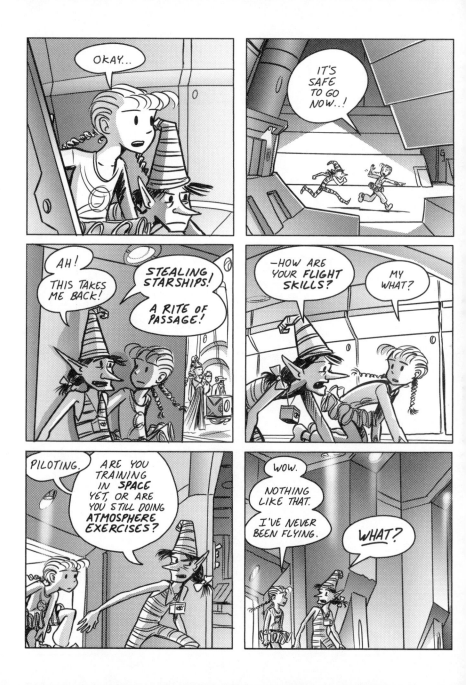

I LEARNED HOW TO PILOT A SHIP WHEN I WAS YOUNGER THAN YOU!
I HAD TO INSIST.
THE HANGER IS THIS WAY...
I'VE NEVER BEEN UP HERE ON MY OWN BEFORE.
≡TSK≡
-YOU SHOULD HAVE YOUR FATHER TEACH YOU.
-IT'S APPALLING THAT HE HAS NOT DONE SO ALREADY!
MY DAD SAYS FLYING ISN'T FOR GIRLS.
NONSENSE!
IT'S ESSENTIAL FOR SURVIVAL!
-ESPECIALLY AMONG THE NOBILITY!
WHY, YOU NEVER KNOW WHEN SOME CUT-THROAT INSANITY WILL BREAK OUT!
UM...
-I THINK WE SHOULD TRY TO BE QUIET.
OKAY,
THIS IS THE STAR SHIP HANGER.
AH!
THIS WILL DO NICELY!
COME ON! WE'LL ESCAPE IN THAT FAST ONE.

CHAPTER TWO

"EDUCATION"

YEAH...
I GUESS WE DIDN'T REALLY BRING ANY MONEY OR FOOD WITH US.
BAH!
-ALL WE NEED IS OUR WITS!
-WHY, BETWEEN YOU AND ME, WE COULD OWN THIS WHOLE DUMP BY THE END OF THE WEEK!
REALLY?
THIS WHOLE SPACE STATION?
SURE!
-I DIDN'T GET TO BE QUEEN OF THE GALAXY ON GOOD LOOKS, YOU KNOW!
GOSH.
WHAT WOULD WE DO WITH A WHOLE SPACE-STATION?
SADLY, WE'LL NEVER KNOW.
-WITH THE IMPERIAL FLEET BREATHING DOWN OUR NECKS, EXPEDIENCY IS MAKING OTHER DEMANDS!
LIKE WHAT?
-LIKE SELLING OUR STOLEN SHIP AND SMUGGLING OURSELVES OUT OF HERE IN A CARGO FREIGHTER BEFORE SOMEBODY— —UM...?
OH...
-SORRY, KID.
FEELING HOMESICK?
YES, BUT I WAS FEELING THAT BEFORE I MET YOU.
-I JUST WISH MY PARENTS COULD BE HERE.
I'VE NEVER BEEN ON A SIGHT-SEEING HOLIDAY WITH THEM BEFORE.

STAND DOWN, SOLDIERS!
GASP!
-IT'S AN IMPERIAL GUARD!
UGH.
YOUR HIGHNESS! -I SCOURED THE GALAXY, SEEKING YOU!
THANK GOODNESS YOU ARE SAFE!
ASHELLE, MEET GRODEN, -MY LOYAL BODYGUARD.
I WAS THE ONLY ONE WHO BELIEVED YOU STILL LIVED!
THAT'S BECAUSE YOU WERE THE ONLY ONE WITH A BRAIN IN THAT WHOLE CRACKER HOUSE.
I SWITCHED BODIES NINE TIMES TRYING TO HIDE FROM YOU.
YOU MUST COME BACK, MY LADY!
-THE EMPIRE HAS FALLEN INTO WICKED HANDS!
NO WAY!
I'M DONE PLAYING QUEEN!
-I PUT IN THREE HUNDRED YEARS ALREADY!
IF PEOPLE CAN'T FIGURE OUT HOW TO PLAY NICE IN THREE CENTURIES, THEN I GIVE UP!
BUT, YOUR HIGHNESS..!
I DON'T THINK SHE LIKED BEING THE QUEEN.
-SHE HAS LOTS OF GRUMPY STORIES ABOUT IT.
I WAS LOSING MY EDGE!
-MY BRAIN WAS TURNING TO MUSH!

CHAPTER THREE

"REST AND REUNUION"

BUT JEN.., I DO FIND IT ODD THAT THE WHOLE TOWN GOT COVERED IN ICE SINCE I LEFT.
YOUR PLANET SURE SPINS ON AN ANGLE!
WHAT?
I READ ALL ABOUT THE PROGRESSION OF THE SEASONS, BUT ACTUALLY SEEING WINTER IN PERSON SURE IS WEIRD.
MOST PLANETS DON'T SPIN CROOKED, YOU KNOW.
THEY SPIN STRAIGHT.
I GUESS I NEVER THOUGHT ABOUT IT BEFORE.
OH!
—DO YOU THINK I'LL NEED EXTRA BLANKETS?
PROBABLY.
—I CAN LEND YOU A SWEATER IF YOU—
JEN! —I FEEL BAD ABOUT TOM!
HE WAS REALLY SHIVERING AFTER I HID ALL HIS CLOTHES IN A SNOWBANK.
WHAT? —OH, HE FORGAVE YOU. —HE WAS HAPPY TO SEE YOU.
BUT I PROMISED MYSELF TO BE MORE CONSIDERATE.
—MAKING SOMEBODY WALK AROUND NAKED IN THE WINTER ISN'T CONSIDERATE AT ALL!
IT WAS SUPPOSED TO BE A FUN GAME, BUT I FORGOT ABOUT THE CROOKED SPIN.
UM... YOU SEEM MORE LOOPY THAN NORMAL.
WHEN DID YOU LAST SLEEP?

IT'S A LONG LIST.

I HAVE SOMETHING HERE CALLED "SLEDDING".

OH, AWESOME! LET ME GO AND CHECK THE GARAGE.

—I'LL BE STRAIGHT BACK!

YIKES! THIS CARPET REALLY IS CRAZY!

ARGH!

WHAT ARE YOU TWO DOING?

ASHELLE IS ON A QUEST TO EXPERIENCE WINTER.

AH. —A CRASH COURSE?

I DINK BY LIBS AH FOZEN.

UM... MAYBE WE SHOULD SKIP AHEAD TO "HOT CHOCOLATE."

OTAY.

-ASHELLE, I HAVE TO SAY.., I'D HAVE BEEN REALLY JEALOUS IF IT WAS ME WHO CAME BACK AND FOUND YOU DATING MY BOYFRIEND.
ARE YOU SURE YOU'RE OKAY WITH IT?
YUP!
WHY?
WELL...
-PEOPLE THINK THEY HAVE TO FEEL JEALOUSY. -LIKE IT'S A LAW OF GRAVITY OR SOMETHING.
BUT REALLY, IT'S A CHOICE.
-NOT AN EASY CHOICE, BUT THAT'S ON PURPOSE.
-JEALOUSY WAS GENETICALLY IMPLANTED IN THE SPECIES AS A BEHAVIOR CONTROL MECHANISM.
AND NOT JUST HERE.
-HUMANOIDS ALL ACROSS THE GALAXY HAVE BEEN MODIFIED.
THAT'S REALLY SUSPICIOUS, DON'T YOU THINK?
I THINK IT'S SUSPICIOUS!
I CAN'T SAY I'VE HEARD THAT BEFORE.
-WHERE EXACTLY DID YOU GO WHEN YOU LEFT THIS PLANET?
I CAN'T REMEMBER.

WHY DOES THAT NOT SURPRISE ME?
OH! –CAN I SEE THE SPECIAL COLOURED PENCILS YOU BOUGHT FOR YOUR ART CLASS?
THEY'RE SO BEAUTIFUL!
–AND I CAN JOIN THE CLASS TOO?
WHY DO I GET THE FEELING THINGS ARE GOING TO GET WEIRD AROUND HERE AGAIN..?
ZZZ
..?
WHAT THE..?!
ASHELLE!!
GOOD MORNING!

CHAPTER FOUR

"NEW ADVENTURES"

HA HA!
I AM NOT FROM YOUR WORLD.
NOR THIS ONE.
NOT ANYMORE...
OH.
THAT SOUNDS SORT OF OMINOUS.
-LOOK, I WAS JUST TRYING TO SPEND SOME RELAXING TIME IN NATURE AFTER MANY HECTIC DAYS FILLED WITH UPHEAVALS.
-I'M NOT REALLY LOOKING FOR ANY WEIRD ADVENTURES WITH TALKING QUADRUPEDS
-NO OFFENSE.
NONE TAKEN.
I ONLY WISHED TO MEET YOU IN PERSON.
AND TO DELIVER A MESSAGE.
A MESSAGE?
HM... WELL,
-THAT SOUNDS EASY, I GUESS.
IT IS THIS...
OH NO!
IS SHE OKAY?
-YOUR FRIEND, THE RED WARRIOR, IS IN SERIOUS TROUBLE.
SHE NEEDS YOUR HELP.
WAIT-
WHO?
-I DON'T KNOW ANYONE CALLED...
HOLD ON!
THIS SOUNDS LIKE AN ADVENTURE!
I JUST EXPLAINED;
-I'M TRYING TO HAVE AN AFTERNOON OF QUIET ACTIVITY!

WHAT?

—CAN YOU PLEASE FOCUS ON **ONE THING** FOR MORE THAN LIKE FIVE SECONDS?!

NOT USUALLY.

I THINK I MIGHT BE A <u>MULTI-TASKER</u>.

WHAT DO YOU THINK?

I THINK THAT'S JUST AN EXCUSE FOR BEING—

HIS NAME IS <u>DANIEL</u>.

HE HAD VERY NICE BROWN EYES.

HE SAID I WAS CUTE.

IS CUTE GOOD?

ARGH!

SO, ASHELLE...
WHERE ARE YOU FROM?
–I CAN'T PLACE YOUR ACCENT.
I HOPE YOU WON'T MIND IF I DON'T TALK ABOUT THAT.
–I'M SUPPOSED TO BE KEEPING A LOW PROFILE.
EXCUSE ME?
–HER FAMILY IS CONNECTED TO GOVERNMENT STUFF.
OH...
SEE, THE THING IS, IF OTHER JEN IS THIS RED WARRIOR PERSON... AND IF SHE'S IN TROUBLE, THEN WHAT AM I SUPPOSED TO DO ABOUT IT?
OH, SO NOW YOU WANT TO TALK ABOUT IT?
YES.
–I'VE BEEN PONDERING, AND THE WEIGHT OF THE PROBLEM HAS SETTLED ON ME.
WELL, YOU SURE PICKED A GREAT PLACE TO GET SETTLED.
I AGREE.
–I DO MY BEST THINKING WHEN I'M SURROUNDED BY LOTS OF STIMULI.
UH... SO...,
ARE YOU ENROLLED IN UNIVERSITY?
ACTUALLY, I DON'T KNOW.
–AFTER I BLEW UP THEIR STARPORT, YOU'D THINK THEY'D CANCEL MY ENROLLMENT.
EXCEPT MY SCHOOL WAS ALSO A BIT CLINGY.
–KIND OF LIKE PRISON.

NOT A TIME MACHINE.
TIME IS AN ILLUSION.
WHOA, WHOA! -HOLD ON!
-ARE YOU SAYING THAT DIMENSIONAL REALITY CAN BE ABRIDGED?
WHAT DO YOU MEAN, "TROOPS"?
-I HAVE A TEAM OF SPECIAL SOLDIERS I TRAINED FOR THIS KIND OF THING.
-I REMEMBERED MORE OF WHAT I DID AFTER I LEFT EARTH LAST SUMMER.
OH, NOW HOLD ON..!
IF UNSTABLE GRAVITY WAVES CAN BE INVERTED...
YOU WERE TRAINING SOLDIERS?
YES. -MY THIRD ARMADA.
-I NEED TO CONTACT THEM..!
BUT HOW?
OH WOW..! -I THINK I GET IT..!
UGH!
-MY MEMORIES ARE ALL BLOCKED! -THIS IS FRUSTRATING!
BUT HALF THE PARTS I'D NEED CAN'T EVEN EXIST IN THIS DIMENSION...

ALL IS NOW.
THERE IS NO "TIME".
WHATEVER.
-AND IT TOLD YOU THAT YOUR WEIRD FRIEND WITH THE SWORD IS IN TROUBLE?
OTHER JEN.
-AN AGENT OF THE LIGHT SIDE.
...
THE WHAT?
WATCH "STAR WARS".
-LOCAL MYTHOLOGY FOR THIS PLANET.
BUT SKIP THE LATER FILMS.
THEY GOT THUMBS DOWN.
OH...
-AND WHILE YOU WERE OFF ON YOUR LITTLE SUMMER JAUNT, YOU JUST HAPPENED TO AMASS ANOTHER WHOLE GALACTIC ARMADA?
A SECRET ONE
-THE BATTLE AGAINST THE EMPIRE IS SMALL CARROTS.
...
SMALL CARROTS?
YES.
I'VE DISCOVERED THAT THERE'S SOMETHING MUCH MORE IMPORTANT GOING ON!
UGH!
IT'S "SMALL POTATOES".
GET YOUR EUPHEMISMS RIGHT IF YOU'RE GOING TO USE THEM!
REALLY?
BUT THEY'RE BOTH ROOT VEGETABLES.

CHAPTER FIVE

"SPECIAL FORCES"

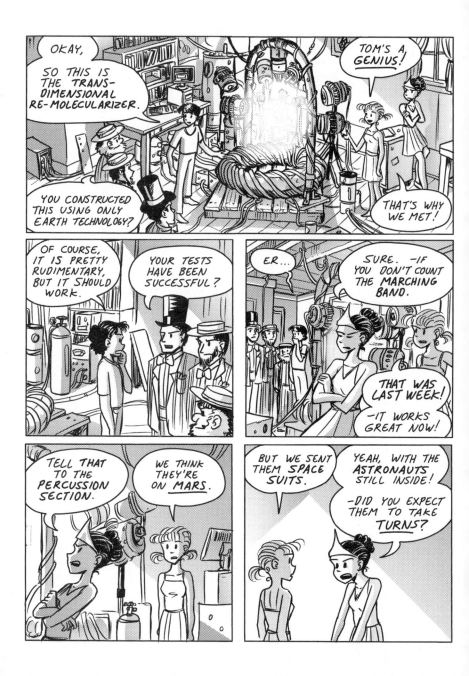

IT DOESN'T MATTER. —TOM'S WORKING ON UN-DOING THE EVENT BEFORE IT EVER HAPPENED.
THAT'S THE WHOLE POINT!
—WE CAN USE THIS MACHINE TO FIX THINGS!
YOU HAVE OUR UTMOST CONFIDENCE, MY LADY!
INDEED!
WE ARE WITHOUT FEAR!
OH, BROTHER!
IT'LL WORK!
—ANYWAY THIS MISSION IS REALLY IMPORTANT!
I CHOSE THIS TEAM BECAUSE THEY ARE MY MOST LOYAL AND CAPABLE SOLDIERS.
YOU PICKED THEM OUT ALL BY YOURSELF, DID YOU?
KYTANNA!
YOUR DISPARAGING REMARKS ARE NOT USEFULL!
NEITHER IS YOUR CRAZY DEVICE!!
ASHELLE! THINK!
—YOU'RE ABOUT TO SEND PEOPLE WHO TRUST AND ADORE YOU THROUGH A SPACE-TIME FOOD PROCESSOR!
IT'S NOT A FOOD PROCESSOR,
—AND ANYWAY, I'M GOING WITH THEM!
WHAT?!
OUR LADY IS BEYOND REPROACH.
THBBT
POW
OOOPS! I CAN FIX IT!

OH, HI, KYTANNA.
-HEY, MAYBE YOU CAN HELP ME..?
ASHELLE ASKED ME TO LOOK AFTER HER THREE ALIEN SOLDIER FRIENDS...
BAH.
-YOU MEAN, ZEALOTS FROM THE CULT OF ASHELLE.
UM, YEAH..,
DO YOU THINK THEY'D LIKE VEGGIE-WRAPS?
THAT GIRL HAS TURNED MY APARTMENT INTO A TRANS-DIMENSIONAL WORM-HOLE LABORATORY!
-AND I JUST GOT THE PLACE FEELING COMFY!
SHE SENT A BOOK I BORROWED FROM THE LIBRARY AND ALL MY SOFA CUSHIONS TO 1985.
REALLY?
-BUT ISN'T IT TOM'S MACHINE?
TOM HAS LOST HIS MIND TO HER.
-HE'S COMPLETELY FALLEN UNDER HER SWAY.

I DIDN'T THINK IT WOULD CAUSE SO MUCH TROUBLE.
DID YOU EVEN THINK AT ALL..?
YOU NEVER SHOULD HAVE BROUGHT ALIEN SEEDS HERE IN THE FIRST PLACE!
I'M SORRY!
KYTANNA IS REALLY UPSET WITH YOU AS WELL!
SHE IS?
WHAT DO YOU THINK?
YOU'VE TOTALLY TURNED HER APARTMENT INTO A DISASTER ZONE!
-YOU'RE TREATING EVERYBODY AS IF THEY DON'T HAVE LIVES OF THEIR OWN!
ASHELLE! WE WANT TO SUPPORT YOU, BUT YOU NEVER EVEN ASK FIRST.
YOU'RE TAKING THE PEOPLE WHO CARE ABOUT YOU MOST FOR GRANTED.
—AND IT'S PUTTING US ALL IN DANGER!
REALLY? IS IT TRULY THAT BAD?
CRASH
DO NOT WORRY, PRINCESS!
WE WILL CLEAN UP THE MESS YOU HAVE CREATED WITH OUR VERY LIVES IF WE MUST!
OOOoOOG.

CHAPTER SIX

"LIVING ARRANGEMENTS"

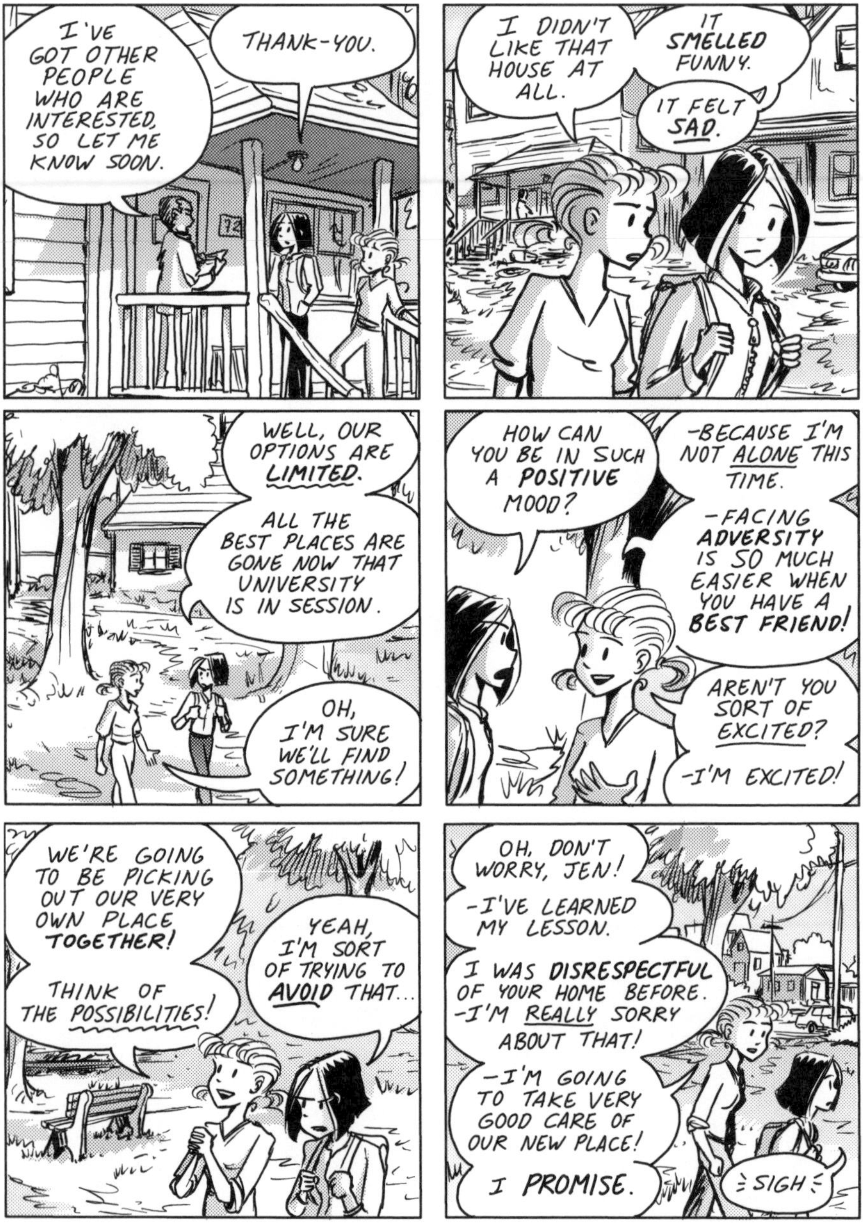
I'VE GOT OTHER PEOPLE WHO ARE INTERESTED, SO LET ME KNOW SOON.
THANK-YOU.
72
I DIDN'T LIKE THAT HOUSE AT ALL.
IT SMELLED FUNNY.
IT FELT SAD.
WELL, OUR OPTIONS ARE LIMITED.
ALL THE BEST PLACES ARE GONE NOW THAT UNIVERSITY IS IN SESSION.
OH, I'M SURE WE'LL FIND SOMETHING!
HOW CAN YOU BE IN SUCH A POSITIVE MOOD?
-BECAUSE I'M NOT ALONE THIS TIME.
-FACING ADVERSITY IS SO MUCH EASIER WHEN YOU HAVE A BEST FRIEND!
AREN'T YOU SORT OF EXCITED?
-I'M EXCITED!
WE'RE GOING TO BE PICKING OUT OUR VERY OWN PLACE TOGETHER!
THINK OF THE POSSIBILITIES!
YEAH, I'M SORT OF TRYING TO AVOID THAT...
OH, DON'T WORRY, JEN!
-I'VE LEARNED MY LESSON.
I WAS DISRESPECTFUL OF YOUR HOME BEFORE.
-I'M REALLY SORRY ABOUT THAT!
-I'M GOING TO TAKE VERY GOOD CARE OF OUR NEW PLACE!
I PROMISE.
SIGH

I'M JUST SO GLAD YOU'RE LETTING ME LIVE WITH YOU AGAIN.
IT MEANS EVERYTHING TO ME!
SO DON'T WORRY.
I'M GOING TO MAKE IT UP TO YOU!
AND FINDING THE RIGHT PLACE IS EASY!
JUST START BY PICTURING THE PERFECT PLACE TO LIVE.
—WHAT DO YOU SEE IN YOUR IMAGINATION?
WELL...
I'D LIKE IT TO BE COZY.
AND NEAR THE SCHOOL...
—WITH A NICE GARDEN AND CHEERFUL COLORS..?
OH! I SEE IT TOO!
BUT WE'VE BEEN LOOKING ALL WEEK!
ASHELLE!
I WORRY WE'RE NOT GOING TO BE OKAY..!
OH, OF COURSE WE'LL BE OKAY!
—EXCEPT, YOU WOULD BE HAPPY LIVING IN A TENT!
HM.., YEAH.
—AND WE COULD PLANT A GARDEN..!

WELL... SOMETIMES YOU HAVE TO TAKE CRITICISM WITH A GRAIN OF SALT.
-I TRIED, BUT THE TASTE OF MY POOR CHOICES REMAINS **BITTER** WITHIN MY SOUL.
ALSO I LET A GIANT **PLANT MONSTER** DESTROY THE KITCHEN.
—AND THE FRONT WINDOW.
WEIRD DETAILS ARE KIND OF YOUR THING AREN'T THEY?
THE LAST TIME THINGS GOT THIS BAD, I RAN AWAY FROM HOME.
-SO, YOU FLED LONELY **TATOOINE** AND VENTURED TO THE STARS.
WHAT? NO. I LEFT **PARISOFFA PRIME** AND CAME HERE.
AH, RIGHT.
-ABANDONING YOUR HOME-WORLD TO THE **CYLON MENACE**.
HOW TRAGIC.
I CAN TELL YOU'RE MAKING FUN OF ME.
IT'S NOT VERY NICE, YOU KNOW.
BUT I SUPPOSE I DON'T DESERVE BETTER.
IT IS FITTING THAT I BE **MOCKED** IN MY **TIME OF SORROW**.
OH, COME ON!
IT CAN'T BE THAT BAD.

MAN! YOU COULD WRITE **A BOOK** WITH ALL THAT **SOCIO-ECONOMIC-POLITICAL** STUFF YOU WERE TELLING ME LAST NIGHT!
-I REALLY WASN'T EXPECTING ANY OF THAT!
-I MEAN, I **KNEW** I LIKED YOU, BUT SHEESH!
WAS I **TOO MUCH?**
-SOMETIMES I'M TOO MUCH.
NO, NO,
IT WAS **GREAT**!
SHOP
I CAN'T **BELIEVE** WE STAYED AWAKE ALL NIGHT!
-I'M GOING TO HAVE A HARD SHIFT AT WORK TODAY!
I FEEL WONDERFUL!
IT WAS VERY NICE SPENDING THE NIGHT IN YOUR APARTMENT.
WELL, YOU'RE WELCOME TO STAY OVER ANY TIME YOU NEED.
REALLY?
THAT'S VERY GENEROUS!
IS THIS THE PLACE WITH THE SPARE ROOM I CAN RENT?
YEP.
-COME ON.
LET'S SEE WHO'S HOME...

I'VE KNOWN A LOT OF REALLY NEAT PEOPLE WHO HAVE LIVED IN THIS PLACE.
-IT'S SORT OF A CLEARING HOUSE FOR THE WEIRD AND WAYWARD.
YOU'LL FIT IN JUST FINE.
THANK-YOU SO MUCH FOR RECOMMENDING ME.
NO PROBLEM.
-GABE, THIS IS ASHELLE.
SHE'S AWESOME!
PLEASED TO MEET YOU.
DREW'S OPINION MEANS A LOT.
THIS IS THE ROOM.
TOP FLOOR. -NICE VIEW.
OH!
I LOVE IT!
I HOPE JEN DOESN'T MIND IT BEING SO SMALL.
IT'LL BE A TIGHT FIT FOR US BOTH, AND SHE'S NOT USED TO SMALL QUARTERS.
MMM...
YEAH,
WE CAN ONLY LET ONE PERSON RENT THIS ROOM AT A TIME.
WHAT?
OH NO!
THAT'S A PROBLEM!
AND THERE'S NOTHING ELSE AVAILABLE IN TOWN!
I'VE LOOKED.
HM.
DO YOU STILL WANT IT?
THERE'S A FEW OTHER PEOPLE WHO HAVE BEEN ASKING...
UMM...
YES.
I'LL TAKE IT.

CHAPTER SEVEN

"PREPARATIONS"

OH, WHATEVER.
THAT'S A SIDE PROJECT ANYWAY.
—SO HOW ARE YOU ON KEYBOARD?
EXCUSE ME?
YOU MEAN TYPING?
NO, NO.
PIANO.
I'M PUTTING TOGETHER AN AWESOME 80'S GIRL-BAND.
YOU'RE IN IT.
WHAT?
—OR, I SUPPOSE YOU COULD PLAY BASS.
DEPENDS WHO ELSE I FIND.
ALSO YOU'LL NEED TO LEARN KUNG-FU.
AM I STILL MEDITATING?
—IS THIS SOME KIND OF DREAM?
HA! LOOK AT THIS! —I KNEW IT!
LITTLE MISS ROCK STAR IS DARK SIDE!
—I MEAN, LOOK AT THE WOMAN!
GRANDMA-AGE TODAY, AND SHE STILL LOOKS 25!
NO MATTER.
—I'LL JUST BE STEALING ALL HER HIT SONGS BEFORE SHE WRITES THEM, THANK-YOU VERY MUCH!
WE'LL DE-TOX THE LYRICS AND PUT THEM ON OUR FIRST ALBUM.
HA!
THAT'LL FIX HER!
BOY!
—IT SURE IS A LOT EASIER TO NIX THIS MIND-PROGRAMMING STUFF AT THE SOURCE RATHER THAN HAVE TO PLAY AT DAMAGE CONTROL.
WHO ELSE WAS BIG IN THE 80'S?
I WANT TO WAKE UP NOW!

JEN!
I MISSED YOU SO MUCH!
I KNOW YOU'RE ANGRY WITH ME.
I'M SORRY FOR BEING A THOUGHTLESS FRIEND!
IT'S OKAY.
I'M NOT MAD ANYMORE.
ANYWAY, IT WASN'T ALL YOU.
IT WAS MOSTLY ME BEING MOODY.
I'M SORRY.
I LOVE YOU SO MUCH.
ALSO, I'M LONELY OUT HERE IN MY NEW RUSTIC LIFESTYLE.
YEAH...
HOW'S THIS WORKING OUT FOR YOU?
IT'S HARD, BUT GOOD.
I'M DOING FARM WORK.
I'M GETTING MUSCLES.
I'M MEETING NICE PEOPLE, BUT NOBODY LIKE YOU.
UM...
WHAT IS THAT?
A GUITAR.
—JENNY MYSTERIOUS PAID ME A VISIT.
—AND NOW I THINK I MIGHT BE IN A ROCK BAND.

SO, WHAT KIND OF WORK ARE YOU DOING ON THE FARM?
ALL KINDS.
-PLANTING SEASON WAS OVER BEFORE I STARTED, BUT THERE'S WEEDING AND TYING AND PICKING.
THERE'S ALWAYS SOMETHING DIFFERENT.
I FIND EARTH PLANTS ARE VERY DOCILE.
-NONE OF THEM BITE OR TRY TO GRAB YOU.
-BUT THEY DO NEED A LOT OF ATTENTION.
SO IN A WAY, I STILL FEEL LIKE I'M BEING HELD ON TO...
THEY CAN'T EVEN DEFEND THEMSELVES AGAINST INSECTS.
-NOT ACTIVELY, ANYWAY.
-SO YOU HAVE TO RAISE THEM TO BE STRONG.
WE DON'T USE POISON SPRAYS ON THE FARM.
GOSH.
IT SOUNDS REALLY INTERESTING.
OH, IT IS!
-AND AT NOON, WE SIT IN THE SHADE AND TALK AND EAT LUNCH.
-THERE'S THIS COUPLE; JAY AND TALLUSA,
-THEY'RE IN LOVE!
THEY'RE TRAVELING ACROSS COUNTRY, WORKING ON FARMS.
AND THERE'S A GIRL NAMED KATIE, AND SHE'S FROM A PLACE CALLED THE "NETHER LANDS"
DOESN'T THAT SOUND ROMANTIC?

-KATIE IS SUCH A BEAUTIFUL PERSON!
SHE'S MY NEW FRIEND!
SHE INVITED ME TO TRAVEL WITH HER TO A FARM IN HAWAII!
-HAWAII IS A SMALL ISLAND IN THE MIDDLE OF A BIG OCEAN.
-AND THEY GROW DELICIOUS FRUIT THERE WHICH ARE THIS BIG!
WHAT?
HOLD ON.
-YOU'RE LEAVING AGAIN?
WHAT?
NO.
GOING TO HAWAII ISN'T LEAVING.
-IT'S JUST THE OTHER SIDE OF THE PLANET.
FOR HUMANS, THAT'S CONSIDERED REALLY FAR!
OH.
I GUESS I'M JUST USED TO INTERSTELLAR DISTANCES.
UGH!
ARE YOU LEAVING BECAUSE I SAID I DIDN'T WANT TO LIVE WITH YOU?
-IS THAT IT?
WHAT?
NO.
-I JUST LIKE TO EXPLORE.
ASHELLE!
-YOU NEVER STAY IN ONE PLACE! -I THOUGHT YOU WERE BACK FOR GOOD THIS TIME!
WELL, I'M NOT GOING FOR A FEW MORE WEEKS.
-I WANT TO STAY TO SEE THE POTATOES COME UP.
ARGH!

CHAPTER EIGHT

"DIPLOMACY"

—I WORKED OUT THAT ONE OF THE REASONS I LIKE THE EARTH SO MUCH IS THAT HUMANS DON'T FOLLOW ME AROUND ALL THE TIME.
IT'S VERY REFRESHING.
BUT NOW... THESE GOATS..!
—IT'S LIKE THEY EXPECT ME TO DO SOMETHING..!
MAYBE THEY HOPE YOU'LL LEAD THEM IN THEIR DESPERATE BID FOR FREEDOM.
ARGH! DO YOU THINK..? THAT'S VERY STRESSFUL!
HOW AM I SUPPOSED TO TRAIN THEM? THERE'S NOTHING TO WORK WITH! THEY LACK OPPOSABLE THUMBS! —THEY DON'T EVEN HAVE FINGERS!
?
THE ODDS ARE JUST STACKED TOO HIGH THIS TIME! I CAN'T DO IT!
—ALSO, THEIR OVERLORD IS OUR EMPLOYER! —I LIKE HIM! GOING TO WAR WOULD BE A CONFLICT OF INTERESTS! —IT WOULD TEAR MY SOUL IN HALF!
UH... I WAS JOKING.
ARGH! IT'S ALL HAPPENING AGAIN!
...

THEY DO?
-I STUDIED THEIR CLASSICAL LITERATURE.
GOATS SHOW UP A LOT IN HUMAN RELIGION. -AS DEVILS AND AS GODS.
THAT DOESN'T HAPPEN FOR NO REASON.
SO...
GOATS HOLD SOME KIND OF HIDDEN POWER..?
HIDDEN?
BRR...
IT'S SO OBVIOUS I CAN'T EVEN HINT AT IT.
IT'S TOO DANGEROUS TO DISCUSS.
WELL, FOR CRYING OUT LOUD!
-YOU CAN TELL ME.
ARE YOU KIDDING?
-YOU'RE THE LAST PERSON I'D SHARE SOMETHING LIKE THAT WITH!
KYTANNA!
GIVEN THE ULTIMATE WEAPON, IT WOULD BE TOO EASY FOR YOU TO SLIP BACK INTO YOUR OLD WAYS.
-AND I REALLY LIKE THE NEW YOU.
YOU DO..?
YES!
OF COURSE, SILLY!
I THINK YOU'RE WONDERFUL!
OH... THANKS.
-IT HELPS TO HEAR THAT SOMETIMES.
WHAT?!
NO!
—I TOLD YOU ALREADY!
-YOU CAN'T CONQUER ONLY ONE HEMISPHERE.
-THAT'S A TACTICAL NIGHTMARE!
HUMANS ARE BAD AT SHARING!

UM... SO I HEARD YOUR **GOAT ARMY** IS GOING TO TAKE OVER THE PLANET..?

MAHHH!

NOPE! —I USED MY **DIPLOMATIC SKILLS** TO AVERT AN UPRISING.

THOUGH, IT WAS **EMOTIONALLY CHALLENGING.** —I SHOWED THEM AROUND TOWN...

THEY WANTED TO SEE WHERE THEIR **CONTRIBUTION** WAS GOING.

CONTRIBUTION?

THEY LIKED THE **PARKS** AND THE **FOUNTAIN,** BUT THERE WAS A LOT THEY DIDN'T UNDER-STAND.

ALL THE CARS AND NOISE CONFUSE THEM.

THE MOST DIFFICULT PART IS THAT THEY **TRUST** ME!

—THEY ASKED IF IT WAS ALL **WORTH** IT.

I DIDN'T KNOW HOW TO ANSWER!

—WHAT'S ALL OF **WHAT** WORTH..?

THE PROBLEM IS, **VEGETABLE LIFE** DOESN'T PROVIDE ENOUGH **ENERGY.**

THE SUBJECT OF LIFE **EATING LIFE** CONFUSES ME.

UGH. **THIS AGAIN?**

DIDN'T YOU ALREADY WORK THROUGH THIS BEFORE?*

NOT ALL OF IT. —NAGGING QUESTIONS REMAIN.

* YES. LAST BOOK. —M☺

≶SIGH≶ FINE.
– SO WHAT HAVE YOU COME UP WITH NOW?
WELL... – I'VE LEARNED THAT HUMANS NEED MEAT IN THEIR DIET.
ANIMAL FATS AND PROTEINS.
– GOATS ARE JUST A SMALL PART OF THE PICTURE.
– SEE, CEREAL GRAINS CAUSE INFLAMMATION.
OF MUSCLES, JOINTS, BRAIN TISSUE. THE WHOLE BODY.
– IT'S HOW THOSE PLANTS PROTECT THEMSELVES.
– AND IF YOU EAT THEM AS BREAD, YOUR INSULIN LEVELS GO CRAZY.
IT MAKES PEOPLE SICK.
MEANWHILE, OTHER SORTS OF PLANT DON'T GIVE YOU ENOUGH ENERGY.
– YOU'RE EITHER TIRED AND VULNERABLE,
OR YOU NEED TO PULL ENERGY FROM THOSE AROUND YOU.
PEOPLE NEED ENERGY TO SUSTAIN AND GROW THEIR SOULS.
BUT OFFERED FLESH PROVIDES A LADDER.
– I DIDN'T REALLY STUDY HUMAN RELIGION, BUT IT'S IN THERE.
– FRAGMENTED MESSAGES PLANTED LONG AGO.
JEEZ, ASHELLE!
SAYING STUFF LIKE THAT COULD REALLY OFFEND PEOPLE..!
I KNOW!
AND TRY HAVING A BUNCH OF GOATS ASK YOU THE MEANING OF LIFE!
IT'S BEEN A HARD WEEK!
I DIDN'T ASK FOR THIS.
IT WAS THE GOATS.
– YOUR RACE IS JUST LUCKY THEY'RE SO UNDER-STANDING!
BAHH!

I KNOW!
-DOES OUR EXISTENCE HAVE ANY VALUE?
ANY PROMISE?
I'M IN A STATE OF EXISTENTIAL CRISIS!
JEN, WHAT DO YOU DO WHEN YOU ARE IN A STATE OF EXISTENTIAL CRISIS?
I DON'T REALLY KNOW WHAT THAT MEANS. -SORRY.
SIGH.
TONIGHT OPEN MIC!
HM... IS THIS SOME KIND OF MUSIC NIGHT?
OH...
WOW..!

CHAPTER NINE

"THE CITY"

I DON'T GET IT!
-YOU JUST MET THOSE GUYS.
UH HUH.
JIM AND HOLLIS.
THEY'RE REALLY NICE!
AND YOU'RE GOING INTO THE CITY WITH THEM?
HOW COME?
I'VE NEVER SEEN THE CITY.
THEY'RE GOING TO DROP ME OFF, I'LL SPEND THE DAY VISITING, AND THEN TAKE A BUS HOME.
IT'S EASY!
BUT YOU'VE NEVER EVEN TAKEN A BUS BEFORE!
YES I HAVE.
WITH YOU. -ON MY VERY FIRST DAY. REMEMBER?
THAT WAS A LOCAL BUS!
THE BUS FROM THE CITY IS A WHOLE DIFFERENT THING!
IT'S EXPENSIVE.
WELL, I HAVE ALL THE MONEY I MADE OVER THE SUMMER.
WON'T THIS BE ENOUGH?

TICKETS
LAST BUS JUST PULLED OUT.
WHAT?!
VIA
YOUR PLANET SPINS CROOKED.
-IT MAKES TIME-KEEPING CONFUSING.
TICKETS
BUT...
BUT...
STATION'S LOCKING UP.
COME BACK TOMORROW.
WHIMPER
I CAN'T BELIEVE WE MISSED THE LAST BUS!
-THANK-GOODNESS THERE'S STILL SOME OF THESE OLD PHONE BOOTHS AROUND!
PHONE
IN THE RUSH TO JOIN ME ON MY CITY ADVENTURE, YOU ALSO LEFT YOUR PORTABLE MICROWAVE COMMUNICATOR AT HOME.
BAH.
-I LEFT MY SANITY AT HOME!
WHO ARE YOU CALLING?
TOM AND KYTANNA.
-THEY'RE THE ONLY PEOPLE I REALLY KNOW WELL ENOUGH TO ASK FOR HELP.
TOM WILL HAVE FRIENDS WITH A CAR WHO CAN COME GET US.
-OR HE MIGHT KNOW SOMEBODY HERE IN THE CITY WE CAN SPEND THE NIGHT WITH.
CROSS YOUR FINGERS.
OKAY.

I GOT THEIR ANSWERING MACHINE.
OH, THEY'RE NOT AT HOME.
-THEY RENTED A **CAR** FOR A WEEKEND TRIP.
ACTUALLY, THAT'S HOW I GOT THE IDEA TO VISIT THE CITY.
-I ALSO WANTED TO GO ON A TRIP.
OH, WELL THAT'S JUST GREAT!
-AND WE CAN'T EVEN GET A HOTEL ROOM.
-I HAVEN'T GOT A **CREDIT CARD!**
-OR ANYWHERE **NEAR** ENOUGH FOR A CASH **DEPOSIT.**
-I SPENT HALF MY **GROCERY MONEY** ON THESE STUPID BUS TICKETS!
I WISH YOU HADN'T SPENT ALL YOUR MONEY ON CLOTHES!
DON'T WORRY, JEN.
WHY NOT?
IT'S DARK.
-WE'RE IN A STRANGE CITY, AND WE HAVE NO PLACE TO STAY!
-I THINK IT'S THE **PERFECT** TIME TO GET WORRIED!
CAN'T WE JUST SLEEP OUTDOORS AND CATCH THE BUS TOMORROW?
ARE YOU INSANE?!
NO.
I LIVE IN A **TENT.**
-I'VE GOTTEN GOOD AT CAMPING.
YOU CAN'T JUST PITCH A TENT IN THE **CITY!**
I DON'T EVEN KNOW IF THAT'S LEGAL!
IT'S THE SAME AS BEING **HOMELESS!**
IT'S ILLEGAL TO NOT HAVE A HOME?

WELL, YOU BE CAREFUL.
-IF YOU FIND YOURSELVES IN A TIGHT SPOT, CALL ME AND I'LL HELP SORT YOU OUT.
YOU'VE GOT MY CARD.
REALLY? THANKS!
TAXI
SEE, JEN?
PEOPLE ARE HELPFUL IN THIS CITY.
UGH!
THAT WAS **CREEPY!**
YOU CAN'T JUST TRUST SOME RANDOM CAB DRIVER!
WOW!
THIS MUST BE THE PLACE!
OPEN
IT'S SO WARM AND INVITING!
HELLO!
WE'RE THE ONES WHO CALLED.
-WE WANT BEDS FOR THE NIGHT!
NO PROBLEM!
-I JUST NEED SOME **PICTURE I.D.**
PASSPORT?
DRIVER'S LICENSE..?
UM...
MUFFIN OF THE MONTH CARD?
UH...
SEE..?
IT HAS A PICTURE OF A **PUPPY** IN A CHEF'S HAT.
UGH!

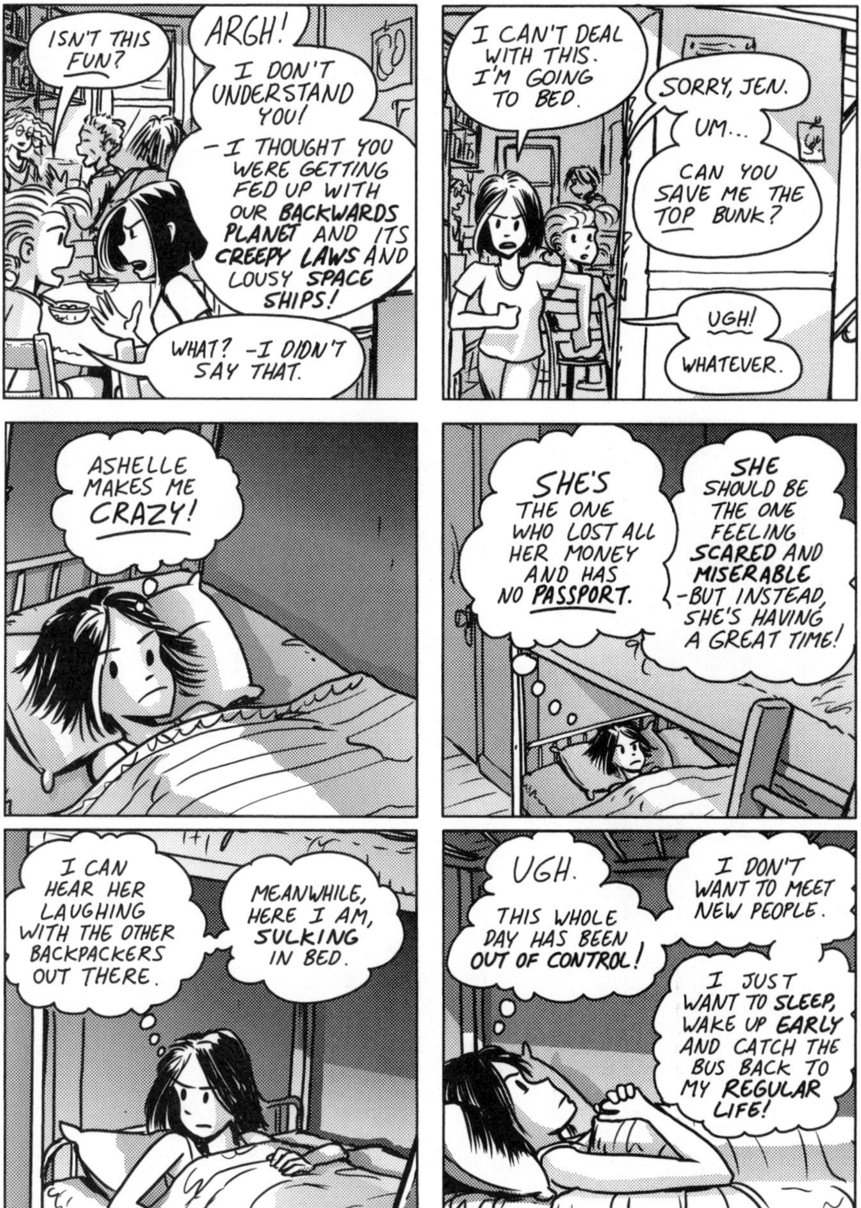
ISN'T THIS FUN?
ARGH!
I DON'T UNDERSTAND YOU!
-I THOUGHT YOU WERE GETTING FED UP WITH OUR BACKWARDS PLANET AND ITS CREEPY LAWS AND LOUSY SPACE SHIPS!
WHAT? -I DIDN'T SAY THAT.
I CAN'T DEAL WITH THIS. I'M GOING TO BED.
SORRY, JEN.
UM...
CAN YOU SAVE ME THE TOP BUNK?
UGH!
WHATEVER.
ASHELLE MAKES ME CRAZY!
SHE'S THE ONE WHO LOST ALL HER MONEY AND HAS NO PASSPORT.
SHE SHOULD BE THE ONE FEELING SCARED AND MISERABLE -BUT INSTEAD, SHE'S HAVING A GREAT TIME!
I CAN HEAR HER LAUGHING WITH THE OTHER BACKPACKERS OUT THERE.
MEANWHILE, HERE I AM, SULKING IN BED.
UGH.
THIS WHOLE DAY HAS BEEN OUT OF CONTROL!
I DON'T WANT TO MEET NEW PEOPLE.
I JUST WANT TO SLEEP, WAKE UP EARLY AND CATCH THE BUS BACK TO MY REGULAR LIFE!

THEY HELD HANDS AT THE ART FESTIVAL.
AND THEY EXCHANGED PERSONAL CONTACT INFORMATION.
I APPROVED OF HIM. –HE HAD A NICE HEART.
I'M JUST GLAD I GOT OVER BEING SCARED THE FIRST DAY
I MIGHT HAVE MISSED EVERYTHING!
YOU DID FINE.
–JENNY MYSTERIOUS ASKED ME TO TRAIN YOU IN THE ART OF URBAN SURVIVAL.
I BET OUR CITY TRIP WOULD COUNT AS A LESSON!
UM...
I ALSO BET I SHOULD HAVE TOLD YOU ABOUT THAT EARLIER.
ER...
SORRY.
YOU THINK?
–START TALKING, SPACE GIRL.
–I'LL, UH, JUST GRAB THESE BAGS...

IT HAS BEEN SAID..,
ALMOST THE WHOLE WORLD IS ASLEEP.
—EVERONE YOU KNOW.
EVERYONE YOU SEE.
EVERYONE YOU TALK TO...
ONLY A FEW PEOPLE ARE AWAKE...
AND THEY LIVE IN A STATE OF CONSTANT, TOTAL AMAZEMENT.
WOW.
—I DIDN'T WRITE THAT.
BUT I GET A SHIVER WHENEVER I THINK OF IT.
ARE WE AWAKE, DO YOU THINK?
I DON'T KNOW, BUT I'LL TELL YOU THIS:
—I'VE FELT CONSTANTLY AND TOTALLY AMAZED SINCE I FIRST MET YOU.
OH... REALLY?
SIGH
REMEMBER WHEN I USED TO BE YOUR GIRLFRIEND?
THAT WAS NICE.
THERE YOU BOTH ARE!
—WHAT'S UP?
LUNCH
FRENCH FRIES ARE A LIE, I DON'T KNOW IF I'M AWAKE, AND I'M LONELY.
SOMETIMES WHEN YOU MAKE NONSENSICAL REMARKS I FEEL STRANGELY ALARMED.

CHAPTER TEN

"SHOW TIME"

YIKES!
JENNY MYSTERIOUS!
AH!
THERE YOU ARE!
PERFECT!
ARE YOU...
ARE YOU HERE FOR REAL?
-OR AM I HAVING ANOTHER 'YOGIC MOMENT'?
NOPE!
-EVERYONE CAN SEE ME.
I'M HERE IN THE FLESH.
DIRECT FROM 1985!
-I STORMED SOME KIND OF SUPER-SECRET UNDERGROUND FACILITY.
-THEY HAD A BIG DIMENSIONAL GATE EXPERIMENT GOING.
VERY 'PHILADELPHIA'.
UM.., OKAY...
-I PULLED A PRINCESS LEIA.
-NUCLEAR DETONATOR IF THEY DIDN'T OPEN A SERIES OF PORTALS WHERE AND WHEN I TOLD THEM.
-I HAD A LIST PREPARED.
SPECIAL
SO.., I HOPE YOU'VE BEEN PRACTICING THE SONGS I'VE BEEN DREAMING TO YOU.
-I GOT US BOOKED AT MAPLELEAF GARDENS FOR OUR BIG LAUNCH ONTO THE WORLD STAGE OF ROCK AND ROLL!
EXCUSE ME?
-YOU'RE COMING BACK IN TIME WITH ME!
-WE OPEN FOR 'U2'!
EXCUSE ME?!

THAT SOUNDS AMBITIOUS.
I KNOW, BUT I HAVE A HUGE ADVANTAGE...
I KNOW WHEN EVERYTHING IS GOING TO HAPPEN BEFORE IT DOES.
-ALL THE BIG HISTORICAL EVENTS.
FOR INSTANCE...
-BACK IN 1985, THEY'RE ABOUT TO DISCOVER THE WRECK OF THE TITANIC.
WHICH, BY THE WAY, IS WHAT OUR FIRST HIT SINGLE IS GOING TO BE ABOUT.
"ICEBERG".
OH, WOW!
-THE LYRICS MAKE SENSE NOW!
EXCEPT OUR SINGLE WILL HAPPEN FIRST.
-OUR SONGS WILL 'PREDICT' LOTS OF BIG EVENTS.
-WE'LL BE ROCK & ROLL PROPHETS!
WE'LL BE HUGE!
YIKES!
I KNOW.
-BUT I'M TIRED OF FIGHTING EVIL DIRECTLY.
I ALWAYS SEEM TO MESS THAT UP.
-IF YOU WANT TO PREVENT PROPAGANDA-FUELED OIL WARS, YOU CAN'T JUST STORM THE WHITE HOUSE AND HANG BUSH JR. OUT THE WINDOW BY HIS ANKLES.
YOU REALLY CAN'T.
DID YOU KNOW THE WHOLE PLACE IS INFESTED WITH INTER-DIMENSIONAL ZOMBIE SOLDIERS?
I WAS SURPRISED.
BUT THE BATTLEFIELD OF MEDIA IS A WHOLE DIFFERENT THING!
MUSIC IS THE WAY!
COME ON!
-LET'S FIND YOU SOME SPANDEX AND HAIR SPRAY!
OH BOY...

—DO YOU REALIZE HOW HARD IT IS FOR ME JUST TO BE HERE WITH YOU RIGHT NOW?
WHAT?
—HANGING OUT WITH A TIME-TRAVELING NINJA GIRL IS CHALLENGING?
HEH.
YEAH,
I'D WORKED THAT ONE OUT.
OH, SWEETIE, I KNOW I'M PUSHING YOU HARD.
—I KNOW HOW MUCH THIS IS COSTING YOU.
AND I ALSO KNOW HOW MUCH HARDER IT'S GOING TO GET.
BUT, BELIEVE IT OR NOT, YOU'RE ACTUALLY VERY WELL SUITED FOR THIS.
—MORE SO THAN YOU THINK.
I MEAN...,
SPACE PRINCESSES?
ALIEN MENACES?
—AND YET YOU HAVEN'T BLANKED OUT A SINGLE PART OF IT.
YOU REMEMBER EVERYTHING.
—BECAUSE YOU LET THINGS AFFECT YOU.
BUT IT'S MORE THAN JUST THAT...
—THE QUALITIES WHICH MAKE YOU INTROVERTED ARE DIRECTLY LINKED TO YOUR ABILITY TO CONNECT ACROSS REALITIES.
THERE ARE VERY FEW PEOPLE I COULD BE HAVING THIS CONVERSATION WITH.
SOCKS
THOUGH...
≡AHEH≡
I HAVEN'T ACTUALLY ASKED IF YOU WANT TO BE PART OF MY PLANS.
I JUST SORT OF ASSUMED...
—THAT'S KIND OF AN EXTROVERT THING, ISN'T IT?
SORRY.
THAT'S OKAY.
I'M STILL HERE, AREN'T I?
...WEARING CLOWN CLOTHES.
≥TCH≤
THE EIGHTIES.
YEAH, THAT PART YOU KIND OF JUST HAVE TO ROLL WITH...

YOU'LL BE FINE.
-GOT EVERYTHING?
OH!
MY GUITAR!
IT NEEDS FRESH STRINGS.
I WAS GOING TO BUY MORE TODAY.
RIGHT.
NEW STRINGS.
NO PROBLEM.
-I CAN GET THOSE IN THE EIGHTIES.
DO YOU NEED ANYTHING ELSE?
UM...
OH! JEEZ!
I ALMOST FORGOT.
YOU HAVE TO EMPTY YOUR POCKETS.
YEAH, SEE?
FLASHING THIS FUTURE MONEY COULD CAUSE PROBLEMS.
SO, NOTHING MINTED AFTER 1985.
-ACTUALLY, BETTER LEAVE IT ALL, JUST TO BE SAFE.
SHOOOM!
AH!
RIGHT ON SCHEDULE.
JUST STEP THROUGH.
I'LL BE RIGHT BEHIND YOU.
OKAY...
GOOD LUCK!
I LOVE YOU!
I BELIEVE IN YOU!

SHOOOP
UM...
AREN'T YOU SUPPOSED TO GO WITH HER?
SHE'LL BE FINE.
YOU AND I HAVE THINGS TO DO.
COME ON.
LET'S GO GET POPSICLES OR SOMETHING.
POPSICLES?
OR ICE-CREAM.
I DUNNO.
IT'S UP TO YOU.
NOW JUST HOLD ON A MOMENT!
YOU JUST SENT MY BEST FRIEND THROUGH SOME KIND OF HYPER-DIMENSIONAL PORTAL!
-ALL BY HERSELF!
YES?
WELL, YOU SAID YOU WOULD BE FOLLOWING RIGHT BEHIND HER!
SHE TRUSTED YOU!
IT'S NOT NICE TO LIE ABOUT THINGS LIKE THAT!!

BUT...
I'M THE ONE WHO PLANNED ALL THE GATES.
DOESN'T THAT COUNT?
NO!
YOU'RE NOT GETTING IT!
-JENNY, YOU'RE SMARTER THAN THIS!
OH GOD.
I'M SORRY!
BUT AT LEAST YOU AGREED TO TRAIN HER IN KUNG-FU AND URBAN SURVIVAL!
SHE'LL BE OKAY UNTIL WE FIGURE THIS OUT!
OOOH...
WHAT IS KUNG-FU ANYWAY?
SO, I WENT TO-
ER..,
WHY IS OUR DOOR OPEN?
4
WELCOME!
ASHELLE!?
SORRY! -WE BROKE IN.
IT'S AN EMERGENCY!
WE NEEDED TOM'S MACHINE.
-AND, BOY, AM I EVER GLAD YOU CAME HOME!
WE DON'T KNOW HOW TO MAKE IT WORK!
WHOA! IT'S YOU!
OH NO YOU DON'T!
NOT AGAIN!
YOU ARE NOT TURNING OUR APARTMENT INTO A TIME-TRAVEL LABORATORY!

...SO I'LL GO INTO DEEP MEDITATION AND ESTABLISH A CONNECTION WITH JEN.
ONCE I KNOW WHERE SHE IS, YOU DO YOUR MIND MELD THINGY AND-
TOM!
KYTANNA!
YOU'RE BACK!
OH, GOOD!
THE HARDWARE STORE HAD THE PARTS WE NEED.
HEY, YOUR SPACE NINJAS SHOWED UP! AWESOME!
GREETINGS, ENGINEER!
I ALWAYS WONDERED WHAT HAPPENED TO YOU GUYS.
DID YOU LEAVE THE PLANET OR SOMETHING?
NAY.
-WE RETREATED INTO THE WILDS OF THIS WORLD, AND THERE AWAITED THE PRINCESS' SUMMONS!
AND WE ATE A LOT OF FISH.
INDEED. -RATHER TOO MUCH, IF YOU ASK ME.
WHAT'S THAT SMELL?
MY BODY ODOR IS ALTERED AS A RESULT OF THE EARTH DIET.
I APOLOGIZE.
BAH!
WE ARE BROTHERS IN ARMS!
BONDED BY COMMON TRAVAIL!
YOUR DREAD STENCH WILL NEVER DIM OUR SPIRIT!
WELL.., A BATH MIGHT NOT BE A BA
NEVER!
ENOUGH CHIT-CHAT!
-THE LONGER WE ACCLIMATE TO JEN BEING GONE, THE HARDER IT WILL BE TO BRING HER BACK!
RIGHT!

SO, THIS THING GOES AROUND YOUR NECK.
IT'S AN ILLUSION ENGINE.
-ONE OF ASHELLE'S ZEALOTS GAVE IT TO ME TO PUT ON YOU.
UGH!
THIS IS RIDICULOUS!
DO YOU EVEN HAVE A NECK?
GLOOB!
STOP SQUIRMING!
OKAY.
THAT'S ON PRETTY GOOD I GUESS.
NOW, IF I UNDERSTAND THIS CORRECTLY, ALL I DO IS THINK OF A NATIVE EARTH ORGANISM WHICH IS AROUND THE SAME SIZE AS YOU...
SNRT.
AND THEN...
CLICK
BLOOP!
HEY! NOT BAD.
THAT'S VERY CONVINCING!
CRUNCH
CRUNCH

TODD! NO!
BLOORG!
WOW.
MEN IN BLACK IN DOWNTOWN TORONTO.
-WITH A COW.
THAT OUGHT TO BE INTERESTING.
SENT!
EXPLAIN AGAIN HOW THIS IS BETTER THAN ME GOING TO GET HER MYSELF...
OH DEAR.
SO, HOW LONG DO WE HAVE TO WAIT BEFORE THEY BRING JEN BACK FROM THE PAST?
UGH.
I DON'T GET THIS!
-WHY SHOULD WE HAVE TO WAIT AT ALL?
YEAH...
-ACTUALLY, THEY WERE SUPPOSED TO COME BACK ONLY AN INSTANT AFTER LEAVING.
I MEAN..,
IT IS A TIME MACHINE.
HM...
SOMETHING ISN'T RIGHT...
YOU THINK?!
-THAT STUPID PLANT-COW FOLLOWED THEM THROUGH!
WELL, THEY SHOULD BE ABLE TO MANAGE THAT.
-THEY'RE HIGHLY TRAINED OPERATIVES
YES, AND NOW THEY HAVE A COW.
I DON'T CARE HOW HIGHLY TRAINED THEY ARE!
THIS IS A DISASTER!

SHE'S RIGHT.
I'VE HAD ENOUGH OF THIS CIRCUS.
I'M GOING TO FIX THIS MYSELF!
NO!
YOU CAN'T GO THROUGH!
—YOU'LL TIE YOUR **HYPER-DIMENSIONAL BODY** IN ALL KINDS OF KNOTS!
OKAY, ASHELLE, YOU REALLY NEED TO EXPLAIN THAT.
WHAT IS A **HYPER-DIMENSIONAL BODY?**
UMM...
ALRIGHT.
TRY THIS...
FOCUS ON YOUR HAND.
PAY ATTENTION TO HOW IT **FEELS**.
OKAY...
RIGHT.
NOW.., FOCUS ON YOUR FOOT.
CAN YOU DO BOTH AT THE **SAME TIME?**
UM...
OUR BRAINS ARE LIMITED.
—WE'RE FORCED TO PAY ATTENTION TO THINGS IN **SEQUENCE**.
ONE THING,
THEN THE NEXT,
AND THE NEXT...
NOW, CONSIDER THAT YOU EXIST IN THIS MOMENT...
?
...AND ALSO IN **EVERY OTHER** MOMENT YOU'VE EVER LIVED.
YOU'RE **EVERYWHERE ALL AT ONCE**.
—**BUT** YOU CAN ONLY FOCUS ON **ONE MOMENT AT A TIME**.
IN **SEQUENCE**.
OUR ATTENTION MOVES THROUGH THE MOMENTS SMOOTHLY, AND SO IT FEELS LIKE TIME PASSING.
BUT IT'S JUST AN ILLUSION.

YOU DO?
HAVE YOU TIME-TRAVELED BEFORE ALSO?
UM...
SORT OF.
-EVERY TIME I LEAVE EARTH.
TIME MOVES WAAAAY FASTER OUT IN THE REST OF THE GALAXY.
WHAT?
IT DOES?
YEAH!
-I MEAN, FIRST I HAD TO LEAD THE REBELLION, AND THEN HELP SET UP THE NEW GALACTIC FEDERATION.
-I WAS BUSY WITH THAT FOR A BIG PART OF MY LIFE!
-EXCEPT ONLY A SHORT TIME SEEMED TO PASS HERE WHILE I WAS GONE.
IT'S A BIT STRANGE, NOW THAT I THINK ABOUT IT.
JUST A BIT?
I DIDN'T KNOW ANY OF THAT WHEN I CAME TO THIS PLANET!
I DON'T KNOW.
ASHELLE!
-WHY DIDN'T YOU EVER SAY SOMETHING?
ANYWAY, I DON'T WANT TO TALK ABOUT THAT.
-I WANT TO HEAR ABOUT JEN'S ADVENTURES!
YOU REALLY DO SEEM OLDER THAN WHEN YOU LEFT.
YOU SEEM MUCH MORE FOCUSED AND CONFIDENT.
IT'S QUITE APPEALING.
WELL, I DID HAVE TO GROW A LOT...
WAS IT HARD?
WERE YOU SCARED?
WHAT DID YOU SEE?
HOW DID YOU BECOME A PUNK BARD?

THE EXTRA BITS. . .

Well, here we are very nearly at the end of the second book! Before we wrap up this volume, however, I do have a couple of neat extra bits to share.

Often in the course of writing *Stardrop,* I find myself struck with exciting story ideas which threaten to knock the plot off course, but which in the end wind themselves nicely into the world, helping to shape things in ways I later appreciate but at the time find a bit baffling. I've learned to trust this process.

"Drawing Democracy" (the three-part series following) was very *almost* one of these, but it proved just a little too big an idea to fit into the normal format. Instead, I allowed it to pop the bounds of the fourth wall and disrupt the story. Readers of Wolfville's bi-weekly *Grapevine* where *Stardrop* originally runs, well they didn't mind, but for this book, it felt a bit out of place. I decided to put it on its own here at the end.

Originally, it was designed to fit in the middle of chapter six, where Ashelle finds herself deep in discussion with a university student, talking through the night about politics and socio-economics and other stimulating subjects. This all came up for me in early 2011 during the so-called, "Arab Spring", a period of high revolutionary activity in Egypt and other middle eastern nations. It *really* looked for a while like the villains would lose and the people would capture power through popular, non-violent means. An exciting time! Many were hopeful, but I found myself filled with nervous anxiety.

"There's so much which can go *wrong!* So many things which need to be understood!" Of course, nothing really came of it. The various secret services active in the region soon exerted control; people just weren't prepared for that kind of craftiness. But for a while there...

At the time I thought, "Maybe some advice from an impartial eye, maybe Ashelle, (who had lived through her own revolution, after all), might be able to help nudge the curve." I made these three episodes freely available on my website for print-size download and open-rights reproduction. They're still there for anybody who happens to smell another Spring Time on the horizon...

MONEY. . .

-WHETHER YOU ARE A REGULAR CITIZEN OR A BIG GOVERNMENT,
THE MONEY YOU EARN AND SPEND WAS ORIGINALLY BORROWED FROM A BANK.
AND IT ALWAYS HAS TO BE PAID BACK...
PLUS INTEREST.
PROBLEM IS...
-WHEN ALL MONEY COMES FROM THE BANKS TO START WITH, WHERE DO WE FIND THE EXTRA NEEDED TO PAY THE INTEREST?
IT DOESN'T EXIST!
SO THE BANKS CREATE MORE MONEY AND LEND IT TO US SO WE CAN MAKE UP THE DIFFERENCE.
BUT THAT ONLY CREATES MORE DEBT!
-IT'S AN OLD TRICK USED TO CREATE DEBT SLAVES SO THAT THE BANKS OWN EVERYBODY!
-OF COURSE, THE ECONOMY IS VAST, SO PEOPLE DON'T NOTICE RIGHT AWAY.
BUT OVER TIME...
-SURE, SOME PEOPLE CAN DANCE FASTER THAN OTHERS, BUT OVERALL, SOCIETY IS SINKING INTO DEBT!
THAT'S BAD!
SO IF YOU WANT YOUR NEW DEMOCRACY TO SURVIVE AND BE HEALTHY, IT HAS TO BE IN CHARGE OF ITS OWN MONEY..!
IT HAS TO KICK OUT THE BANKING CARTELS!
HSSS
DIRTY TRICKS
-YOU SEE...
THE BANKS ARE OWNED BY A TINY NUMBER OF SUPER-WEALTHY CONTROL-FREAKS WHOSE NAMES YOU DON'T KNOW.
-YOU MUSTN'T LET THEM HAVE ANY SAY IN YOUR BUDDING DEMOCRACY!

SCHOOL. . .

DON'T WORRY!
I PICKED A MORE GENTLE SUBJECT, SO YOU WON'T GET IN TROUBLE THIS TIME.
–TODAY I'M GOING TO TALK ABOUT...
EDUCATION AND AGE SEGREGATION!
OH.
REALLY?
THAT SOUNDS KIND OF BORING.
YEAH, ALRIGHT.
HOW BAD CAN THAT BE..?
IT'S TRUE.
–IT SOUNDS PRETTY BENIGN, BUT DON'T LET THAT FOOL YOU!
–IT'S IN MY TOP THREE FOR A REASON!
AGE SEGREGATION;
–PUTTING KIDS OF ALL THE SAME AGE TOGETHER IN CLASS ROOMS.
IT'S A BAD IDEA!
BUT WHY..?
–SINCE EVERYBODY WAS BROUGHT UP THAT WAY, IT SEEMS NORMAL.
IT JUST MAKES SENSE.
RIGHT?
–YEAH.
EXCEPT FOR ONE REALLY GIANT THING...
IT ONLY RUNS IN COMPLETE OPPOSITION TO THE WAY HUMANS ARE GENETICALLY CODED TO DEVELOP.
SHEESH!
DNA? BAH!
LIKE IT OR NOT...
HUMANS ARE PACK ANIMALS.
–DEEP DOWN, WE FEEL A STRONG NEED TO KNOW WHO THE TOP DOG IS.
SCHOO

LIKE FEAR, HUNGER AND REPRODUCTION, THIS NEED IS WRITTEN INTO THE HUMAN GENE CODE.
-IT IS POSSIBLE TO OVERRIDE...
HUMANS DO HAVE THAT OPTION.
BUT IT'S HARD, AND FOR KIDS WHO DON'T EVEN KNOW THEY'RE BEING AFFECTED...,
IT'S UNREALISTIC.
AND ANYWAY, IT'S ONLY A BAD INSTINCT WHEN IT ISN'T UNDERSTOOD.
-IN NORMAL SETTINGS, YOUNGER KIDS LOOK UP TO OLDER ONES, WHO IN RETURN FEEL AN INSTINCT TO PROTECT AND LEAD.
A VARIATION OF THE MOTHERING INSTINCT, THIS SERVES TO PROMOTE THE FORMING OF HEALTHY COMMUNITIES.
BUT WHEN KIDS OF ALL THE SAME AGE ARE FORCED TOGETHER..., THERE IS NO OBVIOUS WAY TO DETERMINE LEADERSHIP ROLES.
WHOSE SHOES COST MORE?
WHO CAN THROW A FOOT-BALL THE BEST?
INSTINCT GROWS DESPERATE!
IT SEIZES ON ANY DIFFERENCE IT CAN DETECT!
WHO IS PRETTIEST?
MANY HAVE EXPERIENCED THE BITTER TRIALS OF THE POPULARITY LADDER AT SCHOOL.
BUT THAT DEGREE OF COMPETITION IS NOT A NATURAL STATE.
IT ONLY EXISTS IN SUCH AN ENDLESS UNRESOLVED LOOP WHEN CLEAR ROLE MODELS ARE ARTIFICIALLY SUPPRESSED.
THE RESULT IS A YEARS-LONG CONDITION OF PSYCHOLOGICAL DISTRESS!
AN EMOTIONAL WAR-ZONE!
KIDS ENTER THE ADULT WORLD WITH A DEEPLY PROGRAMMED MISTRUST OF THEIR PEERS.
-AN ALMOST PATHOLOGICAL FEAR OF RIDICULE.
AND A REFLEXIVE RESPECT FOR THE ONLY ROLE MODELS REMAINING.
ARTIFICIAL ONES.
-ONES IN SUITS AND UNIFORMS.
IT'S A CORRUPTION OF THE NATURAL ORDER!
THERE ARE EXCEPTIONS.
SOME GROUPS OF KIDS MANAGE TO GET THROUGH BETTER THAN OTHERS.
BUT ON AVERAGE...
THE CARDS ARE STACKED HIGH AGAINST HEALTHY SOCIAL BONDING.

TRUTH IS...
YOU ARE TRAINED FROM CHILDHOOD TO TURN AWAY FROM THOSE WHO SHOULD BY RIGHTS BE SOURCES OF STRENGTH AND GUIDANCE.
YOUR OWN PEERS!
INSTEAD, COMFORT IS SOUGHT IN SOLITUDE.
IN PERSONAL "PODS."
IN FACT, THIS IS ENCOURAGED.
WHY?
-BECAUSE PEOPLE WHO CANNOT BOND..,
WHO CANNOT COME TOGETHER AS A SOCIETY..,
ALSO CANNOT EFFECTIVELY CHALLENGE AUTHORITY.
IT'S DIVIDE AND CONQUER,
-FROM BIRTH.
SO...
WHEN SETTING UP YOUR NEW DEMOCRACY,
PUT KIDS IN SCHOOLS WITH THEIR AGES MIXED TOGETHER.
- IT'S HEALTHY, AND IT WILL LEAD TO A HAPPY, STRONG NATION!
-ONE NATURALLY RESISTANT TO CORRUPT LEADERSHIP!
THERE!
THAT WAS PRETTY GOOD, WASN'T IT?
HEY, MARK, DID YOU ORDER PIZZA?
-FROM THREE DIFFERENT COMPANIES...
WITH SATELLITE DISHES ON THEIR VANS?
COME BACK NEXT TIME FOR PART III!
GROAN...

LEADERSHIP. . .

SOME ARGUE THAT THIS IS AN EXAMPLE OF EVOLUTIONARY PROGRESS;
—THAT THE LUNATIC MUST BE RESPECTED FOR IT.
- EVEN REVERED.
1
BUT THAT IS FALSE!
—HUMANS CANNOT REACH THEIR FULL POTENTIAL WITHOUT COMMUNITY SUPPORT.
FOOD, CLOTHING, SHELTER, TOOLS..,
—AND THE COLLECTED KNOWLEDGE NEEDED TO MAKE IT ALL WORK...
IMPOSSIBLE WITHOUT COMMUNITY..!
LUNATICS, HOWEVER, THRIVE ON CONFLICT, SELFISHLY EXPLOITING EVERYTHING AROUND THEM.
AND WHEN THEY GROW TOO NUMEROUS,
TOO POWERFUL...
THEY EAGERLY SABOTAGE EVEN THE MOST VITAL COMMUNITY ORGANS FOR SHORT-TERM PERSONAL GAIN.
THE RESULT CAN ONLY BE DISASTER!
SO...
WHEN YOU PICK LEADERS FOR YOUR NEW DEMOCRACY...
MAKE SURE THEY HAVE REAL HUMAN EMOTIONS!
VOTE
BALLOT BOX
— WHILE THEY ARE EXPERT MANIPULATORS, THERE ARE CERTAIN TESTS WHICH A PSYCHOPATH CANNOT PASS...
FOR INSTANCE...
AN IMAGE OF A BURN VICTIM ELICITS AN INVOLUNTARY RESPONSE IN NORMAL PEOPLE.
—NERVE REACTIONS WHICH ARE NOT PRESENT IN A PSYCHOPATH.
—THAT'S JUST ONE EXAMPLE.
IT'S SIMPLE.
IT'S SMART.
BUT YOU'RE NOT DOING IT!
PSYCHOPATHS MAKE UP BETWEEN 1 AND 5 PERCENT OF ALL HUMANS ON THE PLANET.
—AT THE VERY LEAST, THAT'S MORE THAN 60 MILLION.
× 2 = YIKES!
—TWICE THE POPULATION OF CANADA!

DRESS UP DOLLS. . .

Not all of the big ideas around my studio are quite so heavy.

Some are just plain fun!

I consider now and again neat little items, like making stickers or tee-shirts and such, and while some happen, (I made a whole bunch of stickers which I take with me to conventions), others just don't seem to make it to my drafting board. A pity...

Enter *Margaret Forsey!*

My dear girlfriend at the time, a graduate of a well-respected arts program in Halifax presented to me one day quite by surprise a couple of pages of artwork she'd put together. Paper dress up dolls of two main characters in *Stardrop!* I thought they would make the perfect ending for this book.

Thanks, Maggie! I think *Stardrop's* younger readers will enjoy them!

Dress up Ashelle!
colour-in paper dolls!

for a date!

in the garden!

Photocopy, & cut out doll & clothes. Fold down white tabs. enjoy!

a fancy dandelion-coloured dress!

Jeans & a Tee shirt

♥ dolls created by margaret forsay 2012 ♥

Dress up Kytanna

for yoga class!

fancy dress-up dress!

for winter time!

out on the town!

FINAL WORDS. . .

This book represents a novel experiment in publishing; something I've never attempted before.

Crowd-Sourcing, or rather, asking readers to help finance the printing of a book by pre-ording copies up front so as to get the presses rolling. In the past, I'd always had bank-powered lines of credit to draw upon in order to green light books. Not so this time!

I really think that side-stepping the banks is the way to go in the future, and I will definitely consider this mode of publishing for upcoming projects. If you want to be involved in the future, head to the I Box website at: **www.iboxpublishing.com** to find out how.

I would like to roundly thank the many supporters who made this book possible with pre-orders and generous contributions, appearing in chronological order, (sort of), as well as those who have chosen to remain anonymous. . .

Strange Adventures Comics
Caanan Grall, fellow cartoonist
John Eure
David Tallan, (a Galaxian)
Jeff Smallcraft
Chris Howard, writer, DFS
Ryan Summers
Fred Miller
Mike Campbell, radio adventurer
Max Ink, fellow cartoonist
Trevor Theilen
Ben Lehman

Jake
Jonathan Milljon
Bruce Dienes, photographer
Justine MacDonald
Henrik Lindhe
Andrew Pam, web guru
Seto Konowa
Frederic Eldritch
Dave Michalak
Rachel Blackman
Future Past Times Comics
Adam Pottier

Stephen Geigenmiller, writer, XA
Roland Elyandarin
Paul Gorm
Jason Middleton
Blair Kitchen
David Young
X MacDonald, proud skeptic!
Rachel Provost
Bruno Allard, drum master
Douglas Pickett
Scott Armstrong
Tom Wynn
My Mom!
Elizabeth Brewster
Mark Vollrath
Michael Duggan
Michael Edwards
Tiffany Young
Thomas Jansen
Sarah & Thomas, arts and crafts
Rob Clark, artist & marketing guru
Mark Ottensmeyer, fellow Haiger
Richard Cliffen
Steve Kuhlken
Ariell & Jessie, inspiration for all!
Planet X Comics, from way back!
Christopher Green
Andrew Fuiks, creator
Jay Paulin, fellow publisher
Big Planet Comics
Mark Paraiso
Darin Foy
Grant Armstrong, kilted electrician
Andre Rodrigue, owns a starship!
Jeffery Richard Hildebrand
Joel Nava
Allen Laroque
Terje Malmedal

Sven Wiese
Lucy McCahon, A+ book lover
Sebastian Schwenk
Nicholas Pilon
Ross Hugglund
Kevin Jackson
Kris Lachowski
Matthew Champion
Anthony Lower-Basch
Brian Walker
Erik Soderberg
Mike Kitchen, fellow cartoonist
Janahan Kanakaratnam
Caroline Blay, the girl from France
Mark from Ludlow
James Campbell-Prager
Paul Harmon
Chris Palomares
Randy Navarro
James O'Donnell
Michael Johas Teener
Benjamin c. Hsu
Dave Knott
Sebastian F. Mix
Dave Whelen, genius
Alan Johnston
Temma & Leigh, teachers supreme
Donna Holmes, wonder woman
Jeremy Novak, Editor in Chief GV
Adrienne Thomas
Randy Kee
Abby Young
Bill Zimmerman & Susan Hauer
And the Mulherin Family

THANK YOU ALL. You are the
wind in my sails!

The End

See you in the next book. . !